Secret Serenade

a bouquet of words

Kamalika Bhattacharya

Ukiyoto Publishing

All global publishing rights are held by

Ukiyoto Publishing

Published in 2024

Content Copyright © Kamalika Bhattacharya

ISBN 9789367958148

All rights reserved.
No part of this publication may be reproduced, transmitted, or stored in a retrieval system, in any form by any means, electronic, mechanical, photocopying, recording or otherwise, without the prior permission of the publisher.

The moral rights of the author have been asserted.

This is a work of fiction. Names, characters, businesses, places, events, locales, and incidents are either the products of the author's imagination or used in a fictitious manner. Any resemblance to actual persons, living or dead, or actual events is purely coincidental.

This book is sold subject to the condition that it shall not by way of trade or otherwise, be lent, resold, hired out or otherwise circulated, without the publisher's prior consent, in any form of binding or cover other than that in which it is published.

www.ukiyoto.com

Dedication

Poetry has long been a powerful medium for exploring, expressing, and understanding the complexties of human connections. Secret Serenade is a thought provoking collection that delve into the complexties of human relationships extensively.

Sharing the heartbreaks, ups and downs, joys and sorrows is an entirely new experience. I frequently get choked up when I think about the misery that individuals endure. I appreciate everyone who helped me depict my stories and concepts. I would like to express my gratitude to my family for continuing to support me as I complete my task. Mom, I appreciate how you always smooth out the edges of my imperfections. I appreciate you encouraging me to persevere no matter what. Although I mourn you, Dad, I still draw inspiration from you in all of my writing.

Contents

Heart in Limbo	1
Loop	3
A Silent Conversation	5
Edge	8
Search	10
Rumination	13
Spark	15
Syllables of love	17
Forage	20
Succour	22
Intimacy	25
Sting	27
A Reminder	30
Moment	32
Midnight	34
Lovelock	36
What if I Say!!	38
Candlelit	40
Invoice	42
Tale of love	44
Retreat	46
Let them	48
Silence Speaks	50

Demeanor	52
Pause	54
Perplex	56
Flames	58
About the Author	*60*

Heart in Limbo

You came briefly
And left,
Yet you stayed with me
All throughout.
I regret those
moments that made you
a stranger.
I wanted to forget the
moments when I felt
that my heart is on fire.
Eventhough I kept my words,
Instead of being loved
I begged you for love,
And thought you
Know what I want.

And you never cared,
if i needed you for a little more time,
you never took me in your embrace
when I was breaking down alone.

Secret Serenade

I wanted to write about all those unspoken
feelings I kept burried in my heart,
What if I stand with you and see that you chase
someone else and when it doesn't work out,
What if I say "its okay", "Not everyone
can love us the way we want them to,"
Would you agree or you would go mad
Because accepting rejection takes
a lot of heart.

The wound remains unseen and yet hurts us deep,
Because it's not easy to know that
Someone doesn't approve of what we are,
Even though we are scared of their loss.

Silence being our quiet alliance.
My words always searched for your love,
to turn into a poetry.
The pain absorbed
got converted into the ones.
They never meant to.
A verse, then a paragraph
And a poem too.

Loop

When I slept in those warm arms of yours,
And never longed to wake up
even to whisper those nothings, those were everything.
I nestled into them as if,
there is no other safest zone in this world.
The loop that formed made me believe,
you will always protect me from
Everything dark,
Everything that scared me,
Everything that swallowed my pride,
Everything that smoothened my rough edges,
Everything that healed me from within,
Everything that my world revolved around,
Everything that looked difficult,
Everything that churned my heart,
And yet everything that allowed me to sleep,
With a steady heartbeat.

I saw your shadows,
And I accepted them.

I knew you were not some fallen angel,
I saw everything in your eyes,
Yet I chose to look at the brightest bling,
Afterall, I prayed for this love,
And it is something alluring.

I trust far and beyond there is no one like you.
I always needed your light from
the dawn to the midnight.
The only turbulence in this love tale is
your silent vows of love.
Are they not too tender for my
Throbbing little heart?

A Silent Conversation

Have you ever expressed your love?

Yes, I did.

How often?

Regularly. Almost everyday.

Do you write?

Yes, I do.

Have you written letters to him?

That is the strongest mode of communication between us.

Everyday?

Not really. Undefined timeline.

Do you write poems?

Yes.

For Whom?

For Love.

Do you mention his name?

He knows.

What about him?

He smiles. Because it's a secret.

Where is he?

He is all over me.

Does he read, what you write?
Yes, he does.
Does he believe in what you say?
Perhaps.
Does he read your letters?
He does. I hope, he does.
Does he understand your letters?
Uggh!! Sometimes.
Oh!! So he doesn't?
At times, my heart is so turbulent and emotions are too high that my words are confusing.
Does he comments on those days?
He sends emojis.
Why does he send emojis?
He run out of words perhaps!!
Don't you people talk about it?
We do. I sometimes forget to fight too.
Are you afraid to lose him?
Always. He is my treasure.
That may cost you dearly!!
He is my happiness. I don't wish for other options.
Don't you get angry?

I do.

What do you do then?

I turn silent and write again.

Edge

The cliff and the surrender
will always remain the
highlight of a love story,
And then that clasp of hands
which remains underrated and
ultimately mean so much.
A breath of wonder and anxiety
with clock ticking like
a dynamite everyday,
A wait that never gets over.
It's crazy to fall in love... Isn't it!
While you were busy fixing
the contour of others,
while i awaited with blind hope
That you will know.
Love is a disastrous truth
which can't be denied,
Just with a muffled silence
 that water can offer,
Because we fall much deeper

than we could ever imagine.
To love someone is like wood loves fire,
To be consumed in flame,
To burn brightly despite all pain,
And
Yet language and emotions never
suffice to prove that there is always.
An underneath urge to learn
some ancient language to
describe what it feels like
to be in love?!!

Search

While we always long to
search and find on
ourselves,
We fail to find ourselves
completely.
The way we percieve,
The way we display,
In turn of a smile, a tear we pay.
Have you ever looked at the mirror
And truly try to find the glimpses of you,
that defines you?
If you ever get to see the
amount of battles,
You fight everyday.
The amount of pain you endure
and yet while away everytime,
The amount of patience
you hold, not to shatter.
Every moment,
You will perhaps

Fall in love with yourself,
Once again.
Numerous time when you walked
Through those dark aisles,
Before you give in for others.
You may find yourself on a cradle
Of highs and lows and
There are always those
in between.
When you cried and finally shatter.
You may look at the prism
and see a reflect that
may give exceptional hope.
The multifold of colour,
that bounces back from a
beam of light says it right.
Come what may, there is always
a scope, a moment to make it
yours.
Wear kindness and choose what
and whom to say,
You can stare at the moon
And then decide what it may,

When you feel lost,
You must look at the sea,
A thousand waves all at a time,
Wants to prove their strength,
And yet they fall, all on the shore
to return and rise again.
Life and tide is a messy contrast
And there is always a plenty
to discover.
That's why it's called a journey,
And not a war.
There is always so much more,
And there is always so much to
Write.
Conclusion is not easy,
Howmuchever we try.

Rumination

There are layers in every human heart,
That never surfaces actually.
We often forget that me is
important than the person we love.
And at one point of time,
things change when:
we start accepting the truth,
and start collecting the pieces of our heart.
When you stop making that
effort of understanding my pain,
When you ignored my silence,
When you overlooked my pale face,
When you thought its an endless agony,
When you walked over my dreams,
When you kept me guessing about being loved,
When you never gave me a hand,
When i wanted only longed for you.
When you never consoled me after a fight,
When you never felt it and i had those sleepless nights.
When you asked about my physical wound

and never bothered about the scars of my heart,
Yes, love is probably one way only...
And language of love is often
Unknown and we blame it as overthinking...
Others call it rumination.

Spark

When I met you and realized from the first glance,
How my heart chose you.
And our souls were inexorably connected
In a way that told me undoubtedly
That we were always destined to be
Meant to love each other forever.
So, when i tell you that I'm smitten with you,
I choose not to fall,
but dive into loving you
with nothing held back,
All of me for all of you.
That's the choice I make,
The chance I take.
The forever I choose.
If ever a love were
worth risking it all for,
You are everything
I've always wanted
And worth any chance,
choice or price..

This is our destiny for
happily ever after.
You're the one, you always
 were and will be.
I choose you, all your
jagged edges and rough lines,
Which mesh with my own
flaws and imperfections,
In just the way that
love is supposed to feel-
We found in each other.
For now and always.

Syllables of love

The unwritten pact between
the two hearts,
in separation has a delightful symphony.
I imagine you in every
empty seat, i sit beside.
My love language on days
i feel too cold,
i wrap around your name around my ribs
to keep myself warm.
My love language is a piece of chocolate
that reminds me of the ones we shared.
My love language is to listen uninterruptedly
when you go on.
My love language is to convince myself
even when we get trapped in our busy
schedules and yet i wait for
you with lasting patience.
My love language is to suddenly see
a flower bouquet and send it across to you
without any reasons.

Just to ensure you will smile.
My love language is keeping that
unfinished sentence tucked in my heart
that how hollow it feels
at times on darkest days.
My love language is to stay quiet,
when i want to hold the pounding
heart against all odds that life proposes.

My love language is silently observing
you even when you are fast asleep.
My love language is to stay
mesmerised by our love tale even
though it has whys and hows,
but it is what it should be.

My love language is ' i feel at home,
i feel at ease, i feel complete with you.'
My love language is texting you
'sleep well after a tiresome day'
My love language is believing
you when you say 'you haven't changed'.
Dear love, i just want to say

that if my eyes are on you,
I promise,- you don't have to worry
about the eyes on me.

Forage

Unfold yourself to a day,
And claim your nights.
You are unique,
so, stay upright.

Stop wondering who hates you,
Untuck the people who always gets you.
Don't explain, when you are sane,
differently abled will always try to defame.

Let those comparisons wrinkle down
the towers of blemishes on you,
You are a sunshine, if not
someone has ever told you.
Weight of you will never bother the one
Who truly loves,
Others will always judge the
Length of your dress and hair that unfurls.

Don't spend your time lying like

a carcass in a casket,
For there are morning glories waiting
for you in someone's basket,
You have to archive all that bring you down,
And worry not about those crooked frowns,
There will be thousands and more,
Who won't ever understand you like ever before.

But, remember we have only one life,
So just restructure your emotions
And live like a queen,
While knowing deep within,
All are not important and meant to be,
So, just live and let everything else be...

Life is too uncertain to be an accident,
Believe it, something better has to be coming,
When all your hopes looks like drowning.
I don't know what is it as yet,
Even though it's far from being perfect.

Succour

Bring your limbs together and
Walk down the path,
When you think,
You are completely upset
And ready to give up.

Edit your circle carefully
And let the peace brings light,
Afterall, Life's beauty is infinite,
You just need to redesign it right.
Recollect your memories
Of success,
Even though it's hard to access.
You have the strength to pull it right,
Because you are one of your kind.

Inhale all positiveness
And spit out the bad omen,
Although some people make it hell,
Yet there is always a piece of heaven.

There are people human and kind,
We fail to recognize them and find.

Don't be ashamed of your emotions,
For they keep you human,
Address them right,
don't get them deprived.
Lonliness is not always a curse,
It's an opportunity to recur
everything and shine bright.

Offer yourself the love and care,
That you readily wish to share,
You must know your desires,
They are like dormant fires.
Redefine yourself, and claim
The happiness,
Rest will chase you for
All that brightness.
Everything that shines is
Always judged,
Be a human or the sun.
Stop looking at the hourglass,

It's never too late.

Fall in love with yourself..

Intimacy

What is intimacy?
No one understands
The intimacy of eyes
Speaking to one another,
The intimacy of stolen glances,
The intimacy of handwritten
Letters,
The intimacy of being the reason
Of that song on his playlist,
The intimacy of scribing
Initals of his name on repeat,
The intimacy of feeling the pain
When he falls sick,
The intimacy of praying secretly
For his well being,
The intimacy of wearing his favourite
Colour to feel the warmth,
The intimacy of admiring nature
Like never before,
The intimacy of finidng each other in

Secret Serenade

A crowd,
The intimacy of gently teasing him
And yet keeping the anger aside,
The intimacy of smiling on a silly joke,
And sharing it with himhoping to
 gift him a smile,
Knowing the reasons what turns him off,
And yet the intimacy of falling in love
With him again and patching up with him,
The intimacy of admiring the things
He like,
And gifting him the best even when
The pocket pinches,
The intimacy of looking at the calender
To count and recollect the special days
To wish him always.
Everything is a part of intimacy.
Everything is not physical.
But it strikes the right chord
When the partner also
Catches the similar vibe
Of the longing heart.

Sting

The day we parted our ways,
And were unsure if we ever would
See eachother again,
My feet trembled in fear,
My world turned cold,
My surroundings with different kind
Of whispers,
All about you my dear,
About everything that some tucked
Between their poisoned bossom.
Your departure, and I thought I will scream
And won't be able to accept it and
would break like a dream,
But I allowed the pain to seep into my being,
And chose not to cling.
Although I always thought you noticed,
And I always discovered that you have ignored,
I wore those hurtful stings of words,
That people were trying to hush and
Yet they couldnot.

Secret Serenade

You were scared somewhere,
I knew that when
You told me not to come
for your farewell,
Because, more than my feelings
You were not sure what
if I would burst out
And your image will be tarnished,
But that episode made my anger simmer,
On everyone involved to hurt my core,
I have archived them all like messages
Drafted and not sent,
You always worried about being perfect,
And I always told you that I
would love your imperfections more.
Because those keep us more human
And kind, and rarest to find.
I felt as if my heart was ripped off,
With an unimaginable journey ahead,
Inevitable was the seperation,
Where my foolish hope was helpless,
And for the first time,
I felt the sting going deeper into my skin

And eyes couldn't even blink,
And my heart sighed in disgust,
Sometimes we fail to justify
The hows and whys!!
And I chose silence,
Rubbing fragrance into my palms
And I just winked at the sun.
For we can only hold the hand,
that's warm and kind,
It generates love and peace to our mind.

A Reminder

I can stay when days are dull,
I can hold your hands when they
Are empty,
I can cater to both your joy and sadness,
Bring what you want,
And I would love to comfort you,
I can stay when your days
will be too long,
I can stay when you would
like to get rid of that day,
I can stay when the blue
sky will not excite you,
I can stay when the stars
will deny to glimmer,
I can stay even when I wouldn't know.
What to say, but I would stay,
I may not bring you endless love and
Its true the longer we love the more we lose,
Yet I would stay to see you calm,
I would stay to see you prosper,

I would pray for your abundance,
I would stay untill
You are satisfied and happy,
I need not much but
Your love…
I may not gobble up all the sorrows
Sailing in my eyes,
I may not be able to pluck all
the roses to turn your day pink,
I may not dance to the perfection
To let you know everything is perfect,
But just a reminder,
I would be there
For you, as long as
I breathe.

Moment

Do you remember that moment between us?
Your touch, felt like my blood streaming,
And sending a blaze through each and every cell.
Every star that beams above in the darkest
Of the night sky looked pale,
If only I could capture and take you back,
There was absolutely nothing that I lack,
As you stepped in little closer
Untill I could breathe your fragrance,
Our eyes locked and we spoke in
Silence,
Nothing at all was scripted,
That was the beauty,
To be in each others arm
Was a choice and not a duty.
Our hands, do they mock us?
Between a glance and a peck of love,
Where the world stops,
For the briefest of times.
And the only thing between us,

The mere feeling of the anticipation
Of your lips on mine.
A moment, intense,
Hangs in the air as it pulls us closer.
An expectant passion that kept us
Entwined,
Blurring the boundaries,
Difficult to define,
Where you end, I almost begin,
An unimaginable firework.
That could lit the darkest night,
Our skin was glowing.
And we could see everything
In each others eyes alight.
There are some adventures that
Would never scale off your mind,
Our moment was a sparkle.
And would remain one of a kind.
Do you remember that moment?
That tranformed me and you to "us".

Midnight

I met you in the midnight
Under the starlit sky,
You whispered in my ear that
You've seen a lot of me in your dreams,
So what we are not together
Yet you loved me unparrallelly.

But I told you that night,
You havent seen me when i
Fought with my emptiness alone,
You haven't seen me toss and turn
During the night while I was trying to sleep,
You haven't seen me anxious and then all
That I did to calm myself down,
I didn't wanted anything from you
But only your time,
I never asked you to give me a title
Or forced you to be mine.
In this longing of love,
I forgot to measure what I have

Earned and how much I lost,
I always wanted to gather your troubles
And send them to moon,
I always prayed for a silver light
That would help us soon.
On days I only wished to hear
A longing note from you too,
But you were always calm
And that turned me cold too.

The moon perhaps told the morning star
As it begins to rise,
To take away the fears and scatter them
Across the twilight skies.
Our conversation remained
Unfinished and I turned silent,
But underneath I have
A lot to say my emotions
Are quite versant,
I want to believe in all the promises
Of yours and see your gentle smile,
Know that my heart has travlled a lot
And has crossed million miles.

Lovelock

I got addicted to you as if we were meant to be,
Attracted to you for a thousand reasons.
At one moment,
And for no reasons at all in another.
When the night falls and silence takes over,
My mind tickles your thought and my veins
carry your fragrance all over me.
I can't get rid of your being,
Even when I try hard,
You assimilate to my system
As if there is an unwritten pact,
And you are the last whisper,
In my conciousness before sleep claims me,
And the first thought crawls on my mind,
You look so irresistable in my world of ink and dreams,
Where everything looks so organically designed.
We are poles apart, yet you look so familiar,
As if you were locked with my soul years ago,
And we faced some trials and

Could never get over each other.
I never asked you about your feelings
Though, but they look so mutual,
Even though life has turned thousand
pages and made them flutter.
Our silence speaks volumes
where words are like whispers,
You flow in me like a dream with every heartbeat,
Unfolding tidal joys that's bittersweet.
Unable to conclude the residues,
Promising your traces to be found
in my veins and further deep.

What if I Say!!

What if I say stars are the sparkles and poems

Written by the moon on the midnight sky,

What if I say a loving heart is always afraid of loosing,

Whosoever be they seek acceptance from,

What if I say a calm face hide thousand volcanoes in its burning core,

What if I say my heart longs for another conversastion,

When you remain indifferent and cold.

What if I say your absense brings plenty of emptiness,

And yet I discover you between the words.

What if I say certain things reminds me of you,

And I cant get rid of that hurt by burrying my face onto my pillow,

What if I say the cost of loving you deeply is huge,

And the heart continues to bleed profusely stays without a treatment.

What if the quivering silence starts seeping through the walls,

Waiting for an arm to wrap over,

What if the night sky smears over everything,

And memories looms over those shining stars.

What if I look for a bliss,
And I drench myself in your being.

Candlelit

A silent date. My heart longs for one.
Would you come?
Leaving behind all your baggage of
Assumptions and judgement
about everything.
May there be a small thick candle between us,
A small vase of white and pink flowers,
Splendor white plates and some golden cutlery
Adding to the spark in the dark.
I am little old dated to wear black
And speak my mind even on a date.
Don't you worry for you carry your charm,
I will carry mine,
I won't hold your hand, I promise,
Even while cheering up with some wine.
May that candle flame remain
such that it will weave a story of love.
With eyes bespoke and words at bay,
Let two souls get entangled and score,
Which may entail a perfect metaphor.

May I have you over this candle lit date?
The secret I never revealed is
on the candle I carved our names,
And had lit the flame,
So that we melt into one,
And may I find you in the little nuances of
the unspoken words by the
exchange of glances.
May the emotions stays imprinted in
Our souls fabric,
A place where you won't weigh your words
And may I get the opportunity to
rediscover the safest chamber of your heart.
I will shed those sheer curtains,
A spot where silence won't feel heavy,
And words will continue to flow
And weave a unique tale of passion.
May I gift you a compass
That will keep us aligned,
With a cryptic warmth
Redefined.

Invoice

Don't love me when am happy,

Don't love me when i cheer you up for no reason at all,

Don't love me when i am attracted to that acclaimed self of yours,

Don't love me when you fail to read my eyes,

Don't love me when i break into thousand pieces and mend myself again to walk alone,

Don't love me when you fail to watch me stumble in achieving my goals,

Don't love me when you can't contribute and be constructive source of my well being,

Don't love me when i fight my battles alone and you label them as drama,

Don't love me when i wipe my own tears to wear that fake smile to keep my composure,

Don't love me when you don't like my fragments and get irritated with my fragrance,

Don't love me when you can't forgive and forget my mistakes,

Don't love me when you are unable to accept my flaws and imperfections,

Don't love me when you choose to seclude me even after

knowing that i am hurt and in pain,

Don't love me when you fail to respect my choices,

Don't love me when you abandon my heartaches like just another incident,

Don't love me when you drift to sleep knowing that my eyes are full of tears,

Don't love me when you swear by your practical thoughts and disown my emotional wellbeing,

Don't love me when you are not proud of me and have to keep me as your secret,

Don't love me when you think am just an option and not your priority,

Don't love me when you can't bring positivity and always judge me,

Don't love me when you can't accept me for who i am,

Don't love me when i beg for your attention,

Love me only when you accept my flaws and me

As Unified glory.

Tale of love

I have been fond of fairytales,
The one in which everything feels magical.
I may not have those charming words to capture you in rhyme,
But even then your name brings me joy and a youthful shine.
I wink at your picture on my phone,
When i listen to your voice notes and smile alone,
When others wish to see the world,
I found mine in you, i will always fail to measure how much i adore you.
Words were forst and dired,
Thoughts of you made them melt out and set
Into the lines of a rhythm,
A rhythm that catches the heart,
A rhythm that matches the rain,
Everything in love, always doesn't go in vain.
The dark nights are part of the tale,
Where we learn to overcome the fears,
And rise again...
We reserve trust and frail the monster of doubt,
We contiue to evoke peace and sing our heart out,
We hum the melodies that are lyrical and fine,
In every word i try to find the hidden intent that says you are all mine.
A tale of love always won't have the beautiful princess and a handsome hunk,

Sometimes it's about two beautiful souls who could eternally entwine.
A palace won't define the perfect picture, but our hands together will let people always whisper,
There are thousand precious things around in the world and they are all sparkling and fine,
I found all those sparkles in your beautiful eyes and when they reflect nine,
When i etched your name on my skin,
Our tale became special to all of my kin.
As we always say, come what may,
Let us renew the love and brighten our days.

Retreat

The day you happened,
My emotions were revoked,
The butterflies were instantly felt,
The skin got radiant
And that smirky smile of yours,
Traveled across the line and
bejewelled my shores.

There were days and nights
When I felt blank,
There were worries and my heart nearly sank,
I almost felt I lost you,
And felt the blue.
I looked at the flowers and collected those dew,
And the with every breath, a suspense grew,
I crossed my fingers and just prayed hard
So that our love retrieves you.
My lips trembled when my heart were
searching words to write a note,
I felt the rush on my veins and

had a chocked throat.
I hate how I ached and almost felt dread.
And I believed in the love and wanted to look ahead.

Let them

Let them say what they want,
I am not bound to explain.
Let them talk about my flaws,
I am not going to shed them off.
Let them gossip behind my back,
I am not going to be bothered.
Let them doubt my worth,
I won't try to prove myself.
Let them abandon me,
I am not going to beg.
Let them dwell on complaints,
I won't disturb my peace.
Let them not choose to be happy,
I won't compromise my smiles.
Let them mark their calenders to revenge,
I won't allow them to humiliate my emotions.
Let them settle for less,
I won't stop chasing my dreams.
Let them think it's unworthy to be creative,

I won't stop believing in the magic creativity can weave,

Let them change their choices,

I will stick to mine.

Let them wait for the big moments,

I will live the little ones.

Let them brood over the past,

I will make more memories and turn them awesome.

Let them walk away,

I won't allow anyone to walk over me.

I wanted to feel your heart tender

And offer you mine,

That was the only hope,

Because you brought me smile and shine.

My pen bleeded to express my love,

The words were complex and I continued to sob,

It was not easy to survive those darkend nights,

When you had no option and had to left,

For wanting to be loved is the deepest secret I've ever kept.

Silence Speaks

I never aspired to be anything
more than a dust mote,
But every day the sunrays
brings me a new hope,
And then I got scared of those dark nights,
the days when we had those unresolved fights.
I never wanted to be a mess but a muse to you,
I may not be exactly a dreamgirl for you,
but never wanted to be the nightmare.
I never wanted to be an option but your forever,
Hope you will accept me as your
blessing and not a burden,
My deepest regrets, that you never understood
You're the muse behind every love poem I wrote.
The butterflies enveloped in my heart that I carried silently,
The anxiety of keeping the weight of unsaid words,
And how you were afraid of commitment.
While you pretend to read my eyes
And I tried to learn the curve on your face.

The embedded grace and yet when our eyes met,
It felt like an eternity,
Watching sunrise after rain,
That's why it's love as it makes me feel
Am home again.

Demeanor

I am jealous of your eyes,
not by the way they seem,
That shine with childlike charm,
but by how they hold stories of you,
Those I am yet to know.

I wish i could be that confidant,
Who would know,
Only if i could see through,
those eyes for a day,
I would want them to show me their
cause of pain and heartaches,
So that i may take them away.

And someday,
I would want to trap
All that has caused you pain.
And robbed the sparkle of those eyes,
That is no less than a precious gem.
And finally would be able to tell you,

those eyes shall never be moist
with lace of sadness,
ever again.

Pause

I never thought I'd be sitting here,
alone with my thoughts and missing you.
Replaying all the lasts in my mind-
Our last goodbye, our last hug,
And a gentle touch,
Everything that defines you.

They say it gets easier the more time passes,
but I don't know if I feel the same way.
Losing you has changed me in a way
that I never could truly fathom.
When I want to celebrate my victories,
I have to stop myself…
because all my feelings turn numb.

I may never exactly express,
How deeply it hurts.
The sharp pain that aches
And desolate my heart.
When memories brings me you,

There is nothing I could do,

For certain things we are never prepared for..

And the heartache always tends to pour more.

I choose to put on a warm smile

And make an effort for that extra mile.

The days are long and the nights are longer, but I have hope:

That I will sustain the pain and rise stronger.

And I'll be ready for those memories crashing in.

I'll think of you and hold that grin…

Hope is often the best thing to hold on,

After every storm, right from the dusk untill the dawn.

One day, one smile and one happy memory at a time.

Perplex

The more I started to rekindle the things,
that moved my soul and stoked my heart,
the more that girl came out and reminded
me who I once was so long ago,
And what turns me apart.

The girl that dreamed endlessly,
loved intensely and saw the charm
in everything and everyone around her.
The person that would roll her windows
down and turn her music up,
letting the breeze billow through
her hair as she let go of the world
To let her dream unfurl.

A moment that holds millions of thoughts,
And what we hold close to our hearts.
how I could just feel you seemlessly in places
that you aren't and yet I sense your presence.
Even when you're nowhere near,

My heart wondered and burned in fear.
But that's how it has always been,
My heart remained curious and keen.
All the wishes I made on shooting stars
Which are away and million miles far.
Yet I whisper my dreams to my mightiest knight,
With every happy thought that crosses my mind,
Trust me !! You are my eternal find.

Flames

When the stillness of the night falls upon us,
and serenity embraces us,
As I observe your sleeping form
I couldn't have asked for a better companion.
The world seems to melt away in those moments,
and the cares and concerns of the day,
don't seem to matter anymore,
as I can only think of our love and you.

These are the times that I wish I could freeze,
Suspend time as we linger in loves grasp,
The quiet and still calming our hearts
As we are one, two souls connected as one.

All the thoughts, feelings and emotions
Just seemed to dissolve as we rest quietly,
Your motionless body next to mine,
My heart full as I enjoy the beauty of the moment.

It's the snapshots of these instants

That I'll look back on and always remember,
For these are the memories for life,
That will always mean everything to me..
Forever and always, yours.

About the Author

Kamalika Bhattacharya

Kamalika Bhattacharya has written poems, short stories, and editorials for a variety of publications. She has worked with media houses as an editor. Her work skillfully blends passion, drama, and love. She earned degrees in mass communication and print journalism from IIMC. She has years of valuable professional experience working for various print and media companies. Her desire to travel drives her to write down her thoughts and create a variety of storylines.

She accurately measures the components to make the story last because she is an avid reader and observer. She works hard to convey the range of emotions that exist in human life by providing the characters with appropriate intonations. She writes with passion and a wide range of strong emotions in her work. Her previous solo book Smitten by Love, a collection of short stories and a collection of poems book named Sacred Scoop, Ink and embers.

www.ingramcontent.com/pod-product-compliance
Lightning Source LLC
LaVergne TN
LVHW041547070526
838199LV00046B/1859